For Posey and Clem

Under the freeway overpass,
behind the guardrail,
down by a muddy drainage ditch,
lived Axle, the Freeway Cat.

His home was an abandoned car
with four flat tires
and an engine that couldn't be fixed.

Axle made it cozy, though.
In back was a bunk to sleep in,

and a bureau,
and a hook for his hat,
and a hook for his coat,
and a shoebox for shoes.

Every morning,
Axle woke up
to the sound of the cars
on the freeway.
He pulled the curtains open
and sat down to breakfast
at the dashboard.
After breakfast,
he washed his pots and pans
and hung them to dry
on the steering wheel.
Then it was time
to go to work.

BEEP
BEEP

Axle worked for the Department of Highways
as a litter collector.
He trudged for miles each day,
picking up rubbish under the hot sun.
Diesels, dump trucks, pickups and hot rods
rumbled and roared by.
Over, under and around they whizzed.
No one waved. No one called hello to Axle.
He was alone on the freeway.

But there were always surprises:
hubcaps, mufflers, wrenches,
even a bag of potato chips.
And last week Axle found
the best surprise of all.
A shiny new harmonica.

In the evening after dinner,
Axle loved to sit in the front seat
with the window down
and play his harmonica.

The music echoed off the concrete overpass.
To Axle it sounded as if he were playing
in a great cathedral.
"Listen, everybody! Listen to that!" Axle yelled.
But no one did. They were too busy driving.

One afternoon there was a traffic jam
on the freeway.
Cars were backed up for miles.

They were stopped
on the underpass,
the overpass,
the slow lane,
and even the fast lane!

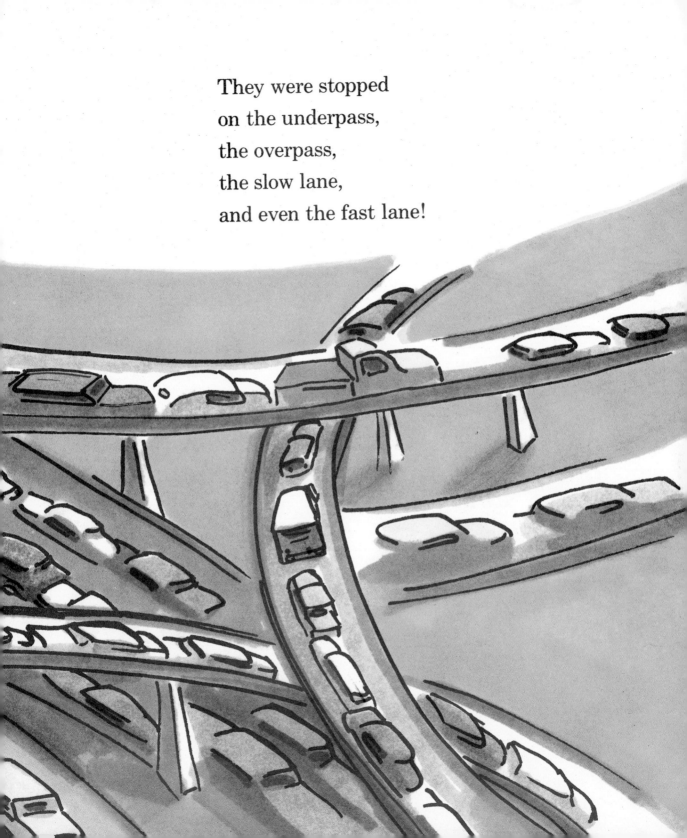

Smack in the middle
of those hundreds of cars
sat a little cat
in a little red car
with a steaming radiator
and a clunking in the engine.

Her car was blocking all the other cars.
Nobody did anything about it.

Except Axle.
He jumped over the guardrail
and opened the hood.
He took out his tools.
He tightened a bolt.
He sealed a gasket.
He fiddled with the carburetor.
And he cooled off the radiator
with a bucket of water from the drainage ditch.

"That should do it," said Axle.

"Thank you," said the little cat.

"Nice car," said Axle. "Does it go very fast?"

"It sure does," said the little cat.

"Would you like to take it for a spin?"

"WOW! Sure!" said Axle.

Axle started the car.
SCREEEEECH…
GRIND…
BANG…
And away they went…

over the underpass,
under the overpass,
around and around the freeway,
until Axle had passed every car in sight.
By then the sun was going down.
"My place is right down there," Axle said.
"How about a bite to eat?"
"Terrific! I'm starving," said the little cat.
Axle stepped on the gas.

"HIT THE BRAKES!!!!" shouted the little cat.
"OH NO!!!!" shouted Axle.
The little red car
scrunched over the vegetable garden,
crashed through the hubcap fence
and smashed into Axle's homemade sprinkler.

"Yikes! What a mess," cried the little cat.

"I'll clean it up later," said Axle.

"First let's have some milk."

"It's cozy here,"
said the little cat.
"And what a nice view
of the overpass.
But isn't it noisy?"
"It quiets down in the evening," said Axle.
"That's when I play my harmonica."
"Really? I play the horn,"
said the little cat.
"Terrific! We could play
some music right now," said Axle.
And he pulled out his harmonica.

And as the sky grew dark over the freeway,
they played a duet
for harmonica and auto horn
down by the muddy drainage ditch,
under the freeway overpass.

Library of Congress Cataloging in Publication Data
Hurd, Thacher.
    Axle the freeway cat.

    Summary: A lonely cat meets a new friend in a
traffic jam.
    [1. Cats—Fiction.   2. Express highways—Fiction]
I. Title.
PZ7.H9562Ax 1981   [E]   80-8432
ISBN 0-06-022697-8   AACR2
ISBN 0-06-022698-6 (lib. bdg.)

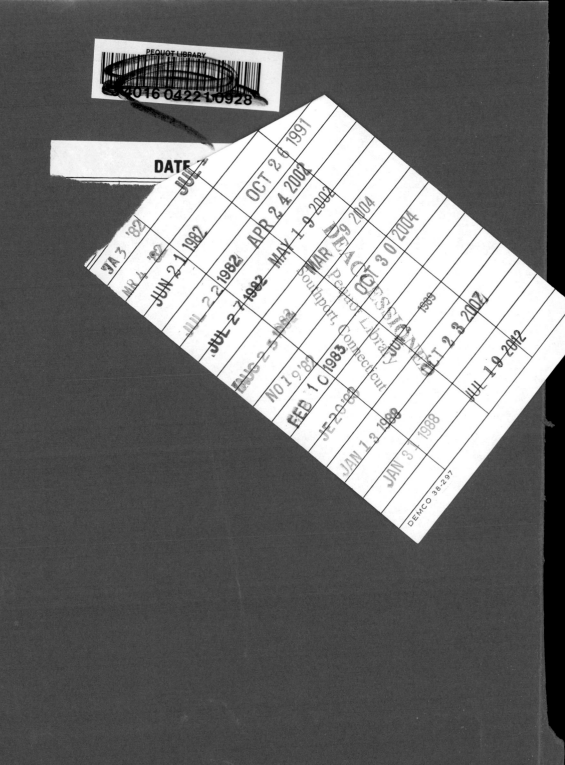